Invisible Ed

by Sophie Wilkinson

Published by JJ Moffs Independent Book Publisher 2019

JJ Moffs Independent Book Publisher Ltd
Grove House Farm, Grovewood Road,
Misterton, Nottinghamshire DN10 4EF

ISBN 978-1-9165042-9-5

Printed and bound in Great Britain by Clays Ltd, Elcograf S.p.A
Typeset by Anna Richards
Cover design by Sophie Wilkinson

Isabella, Mia and India

I hope you enjoy reading
this !

Love
    Miss Wilkinson
        xxx.

Contents

Chapter 1

Just, Ed

You may have read stories about magical places or mythical characters that travel to faraway lands and experience incredible adventures filled with mystery and thrills. This doesn't start as one of those stories. This story starts with a sullen-looking boy named Edward Uset, or Ed as he was known as. Ed didn't have magnificent superpowers of strength. In fact, he was quite small for his age. Nor did he own a magical cape that allowed him to travel at the speed of light away from danger, and he most definitely did not live in a faraway kingdom. He lived in a seemingly boring town named Devantrue, where nothing remotely magical ever happened. But, as you read this story, you will see that Ed, in fact, did experience something that could only be described to you as extraordinary. First, however, you must realise just how ordinary his life had started out.

Ed was ten years old. There wasn't anything particularly special or unique to know about him really, he was just, Ed. He lived in an ordinary house with his mum, dad and older brother, Jack. Mum worked at the local shop and was always very busy with jobs. If ever Ed asked her if they could talk, her reply was generally, "I'm meeting myself coming back right now, can it wait, Love?"

In terms of communication, Ed's brother, Jack, didn't say all that much either. He was five years older than Ed and, unlike his younger brother, was very popular, and very sporty. Jack listened to rock bands, played the guitar, and was captain of his school's football team. The Uset brothers went to schools next door to each other, Ed to the junior site and Jack to the secondary site. Jack would sometimes walk Ed to the gate, and from then on, Ed was invisible to his older brother until they met back at home. At home, Ed felt a little less invisible to Jack, who would acknowledge Ed on his way from the fridge to his bedroom. He hated Ed sneaking into his room and rifling through his CDs, and pretty much thought that his younger brother was the most annoying human being on earth. That was a shame for Ed, as Jack was his idol. Growing up, the two brothers were really close and would spend endless hours in each other's company, but as soon as Jack left for secondary school that all changed.

Ed idolised his dad, and he thought his dad was one of the most intelligent people he knew. Mr Uset could make almost anything out of nothing. Ed and his dad used to build solar systems, rockets, and endless other random creations in a crooked old shed in their back garden. It didn't look much from the outside, but if you opened the splintered door that was hanging on by the end of its hinges, you would discover a universe of bolts, wires, wood, and a busy table at which they would spend hours sawing and glueing, and making brilliant creations. They had gathered so many that Ed's dad had even built a shelf in the shed so that they could proudly display all of their finished inventions.

Ed's favourite ever creation though was far too big to fit on the shelf. He and his dad had taken an old, rusty go-cart and glued a wooden roof to it. Then they painted the entire thing in racing red, so that Ed had his very own high-speed rocket. After school, his dad would push him from the top of the hill near their ordinary street to see just how fast it could go! Not long after the great rocket build, though, came Dad's new job, and that meant that all of the hours he'd spent in the shed were now spent at his new workshop with his new, horrible boss. After that, the only thing he had time to build was ordinary furniture for ordinary people. One evening, when his dad had been so busy at the workshop that he hadn't arrived home in time to see Ed before bed, he promised his son that one day the family would have enough money to open their very own shop, so that he could build amazing creations that he would design with Ed's help. He had promised that on weekends and school holidays, Ed could spend all day in the shop with him and help him build. But that promise had not yet become a reality, and so Ed spent his time alone in the most unique creation that his dad had ever made; his bedroom.

Last summer, just before Mr Uset had started his new job, they decorated Ed's room. If you didn't know by now, Ed was only really interested in space. So, his dad had turned his bedroom into a galaxy. One wall was completely black with tiny specks of white paint splashed all over it just like the Milky Way, and in the corner stood a top of the range, high tech, ten times zoom telescope so that Ed could hunt for stars and planets on clear nights. But the best thing about the room, and probably the most extraordinary thing in Ed's life, was the bed that his dad had built from scratch. A bunk bed, in reality, the top half being the bed, underneath it had a secret den compartment hidden by a small sliding door. Just through the door was a dark cave that held a console, a small TV, and two of the softest, fluffiest cushions. When the sliding door was closed, the only thing that could be seen was the glow of the TV. If Ed had a terrible day at school or felt lonely, the den was the best place to be. It was cosy and safe, and if Ed snuck some snacks in there, there wasn't any need to emerge for hours.

Other than Mum, Dad, and Jack, there was one other very important person in Ed's life, who was never too busy, and that was Sam Cara. Sam had a permanently kind face, the kind that felt like home. He and Ed had known each other since their first day at nursery school, and they'd been inseparable ever since. They did almost everything together and had endless interests in common. Two of their most favoured were anything space-related, and video gaming in Ed's den. Friday night sleepovers comprised of endless snacks and gaming until the early hours, and then, just as their eyes became so heavy that they could barely keep them open, they'd check Ed's telescope just to see, by chance, if they could be the first ten-year-olds to spot alien life. Sam always had time for Ed; they felt more like brothers than friends.

One early summer evening, nearing the end of the summer holidays, the local news reported that the ordinary town of Devantrue was due to see a magical meteor shower. Excited by something so incredible, the boys had waited all summer long and decided they'd venture, telescope in tow, to the local farmer's field where there were plenty of mounds for the best views. After the shower had passed, they had to climb a tree so high (in an attempt to escape Bradley Bellua, the local bully), that they got stuck and had to be rescued by Ed's dad and a very rusty ladder. They were stuck up there for hours before anyone thought to come looking. During their stranded hours up the old oak tree, Ed and Sam formed a secret pact that when life was finally sustainable on Mars, they would both buy tickets and would live side by side in futuristic pods, drive rockets, and wouldn't have the hassle of Brad the bully, homework, or chores ever again!

Chapter 2

School

Now don't be misled, Ed didn't hate school. He shared all of his days with Sam and loved science lessons on Tuesdays and Fridays. However, there was one thing (or one person) who could spoil an entire day with a single word. Ed wished every morning, on his walk up the cobbled school path, that he could be as invisible at school as he was at home to his family, but he wasn't. Ed was in the same year as Brad Bellua and his friends.

Bradley Bellua, as you may have already guessed, was not a friend of Ed's. He was good at almost everything – except being nice to people. In a way, though, you could say that he was very good at not being nice to people. It seemed to Ed that Brad set out to deliberately make his life miserable every single school day. He was captain of the football team and the tallest and toughest boy in their year. He was always chosen first in PE, and everyone, including some of the teachers it seemed, was scared of him - even his friends, the band of loyal followers as Ed and Sam would refer to them. The group was made up of Dan, Callum, and Tom. Whatever Brad ordered, they appeared to agree blindly, and it never worked in Ed's favour. Brad and his friends were the sole reason that Ed didn't enjoy school most of the time. Anticipating meeting his bully eclipsed the excitement of any science lesson for Ed. It was always a push or shove in the corridor or name-calling going into class. Brad's favourite line whenever he noticed Ed was to shout at the top of his giant lungs "Here comes Deadward".

Brad didn't limit his attacks to Ed alone; there were

other unfortunate people whose very existence seemed to irritate Brad, but Ed noticed that his bully seemed to hate him just a little more than he hated the others. Maybe it was because Ed was smaller than everyone in their year, or because he had an ongoing and intense obsession with space that Bradley just didn't understand. It may have even been because Ed was not in the slightest bit sporty. Whatever the reason, whenever Ed saw Brad Bellua walking towards him, he would develop a powerful ache in the pit of his stomach, clench his fists to try and ease the feeling, wishing so much that he was invisible.

As for the rest of school, when Ed wasn't in class he would spend all of his break times and lunch in the library with Sam. They would sit and research space and the possibility of sustaining life on other planets, or whether there really was alien life out there. Space, for Ed especially, seemed so far away and distant from real life. It was so vast, and for Ed, when the burden of Brad, and the ache of missing his dad laid heavy on his mind, it was a welcome escape from reality.

Ed's teacher, Mr Dion, was a tall man with little hair left. Ed assumed this was due to the stress of having Brad in his class. He was incredibly strict and only ever seemed to shout, except for when he called the register, and then the shout would change to what Ed could only describe as a sharp bark. Ed's mum knew Mr Dion quite well, as she had been into school a handful of times over the year to see him regarding the ongoing situation with Brad. The last time Ed's mum went in to complain about Brad it was to recover her son's school uniform, which Brad had decided to take during PE.

Having sat and listened to his mum debating with Mr Dion, his head going back and forth like he was watching a Wimbledon tennis match, the one thing that was etched on Ed's brain was Mr Dion's words of "Sometimes, Mrs Uset, boys will be boys." Mr Dion had promised Ed's mum that he would punish Brad, which he did the following day, but that comment angered Ed. It had created a tornado in his stomach that bolted and twisted. Ed didn't understand how boys were just boys. After all, he himself was a boy, yet he didn't spend his time hurting other people. Ed felt let down by Mr Dion on that afternoon, and for that reason, any remaining enthusiasm he had left for school was gone. The punishment, if you were at all intrigued, was a two-day detention, which meant Brad couldn't go outside at break times or lunches to play football on the playground. For Ed, this only made things at school more difficult, as Brad made sure that he taunted or hurt Ed in as many ways as possible to get his own back. Brad's other target was Peter Tapper. Peter wasn't at all like Ed, but Brad didn't discriminate in his onslaught of terror. Peter was very good at sports and was reasonably popular; he wasn't all that small either, so Ed was somewhat confused by this choice of target. Maybe, Ed concluded, Brad was jealous because Peter was good at the same things as him and was well-liked at the same time.

Science was Ed's favourite lesson. Mrs Hooper, the science teacher, had jet black hair that was scraped back tightly in a bun at the back of her head and a nose as sharp as a knife, and she was Ed's only salvation. She was the strictest teacher in the entire school and had zero patience for anyone, which was great for Ed because she didn't tolerate Brad for longer than five minutes in each lesson. Brad usually did something stupid and got sent straight out, which meant that for two hours a week, Ed was able to concentrate on what he enjoyed most without rubbers being thrown at his head, or being called Deadward.

Since the incident with the missing uniform, the only time of day that filled Ed with complete joy and eased the ache in his stomach was half past three – home time. He and Sam would race out of school and take the long route home. Few people from school walked that route down past the corner shop and the canal. Each day, Sam and Ed would stop at the shop for chocolate and then stroll home. This was a thirty minute journey that didn't involve any worry or anxiety, and it was one of the very few times that Ed felt truly happy inside. Once home, he would sneak into Jack's room before Jack got home from football and play Jack's guitar, although not with much rhythm. However, no matter how hard Ed tried to put everything back where it should be, Jack always seemed to know that there had been an intruder in his room, and an argument would break out. The short time spent in the out of bounds bedroom though was always worth the telling off, and when in there, Ed felt close to his brother again, just like he used to.

Chapter 3

Bradley Bellua

Now, you may have read this far and have already made up your mind about Bradley Bellua. You've probably labelled him a bully and assumed that there wasn't much more to know about Brad. But Bradley, unbeknownst to Ed, would play, in the not so distant future, a very different role in Ed's existence. To Ed though, Brad was just the mean kid who carried an even meaner expression on his face all of the time. In fact, when Ed stopped to consider it, he'd never actually seen Brad look happy. Even when he was hurting someone or playing a practical joke at someone else's expense, he never truly looked content. His hair was always messy and his clothes just the same. Brad didn't walk either; he stomped. He stomped from place to place in a way that made it look like he was about to lose his temper at any moment, and pity the person who was in his way when he did.

Brad lived on the road next to Ed's, so, unfortunately, even when Ed wasn't at school, he still ran the risk of bumping into Brad. Since the case of the missing uniform, Ed felt his mum had given up on advising him about his bully. She just kept encouraging him to ignore Brad and act like he didn't bother him.

"Don't react, Ed, and I'm sure he'll get bored," she advised.

But deep down, Ed knew that Brad would never get bored of picking on his favourite victim. What else would he do with his time, Ed wondered. Brad always seemed to be wound up, like the whole world was against him. He never had a curfew when playing out, so he was a constant threat to Ed from the minute he emerged from his house to the minute he decided he was finally bored of being mean to everybody in his path.

Brad at home was at least less scary than Brad at school, thanks to Brad's dad. Mr Bellua used to be in the army. He was ten times taller and ten times tougher than Brad, and even Brad himself appeared to be afraid of his dad. As difficult as it may be for you to imagine, there was a time, Ed remembered, when Brad wasn't at all mean. His dad was still an active soldier and so wasn't always at home, and it was mainly just Brad and his mum. Brad's mum was a small lady who always wore a smile and would help out at school most days. Their garden was filled with the most colourful flowers, and that was the last time Ed recalled seeing Brad smile. One day, when Brad's dad was home, his mum left. No one knew the reason, but that was the day that everything changed. Brad turned angry, the flowers in their garden died, and the curtains in their house stayed permanently closed.

More recently, Brad's dad would spend most days sitting outside their house on their rusty porch watching the world go by and drinking from green cans. Like Brad, Mr Bellua never ever seemed to be happy, and he had a glum expression stuck to his face. It was for this reason, Ed was told whenever he complained about Brad, that Ed's mum didn't like to bother Mr Bellua. One night though, she had to go round as Brad had pushed Ed into Mrs McCollum's pond, resulting in his brand new trainers being ruined and a gaping cut on his knee. She marched her son round to Brad's house and made him wait at the gate while she spoke to Mr Bellua. Ed observed the anger oozing from Mr Bellua's face. The towering, angry giant yelled at Brad to get inside, and Brad was nowhere to be seen at school the next day.

Chapter 4

Thursday and the bad news

Thursday was Ed's favourite day of the week. Why? Because Thursday evenings were when Brad played football at the school club until 5 pm, meaning Ed and Sam could walk the short way home. Once home, the duo would separate, scramble to get changed, grab bikes, and then meet at the end of the street to go to the park down the road. Ed loved Thursdays so much that whenever he was battling the aching feeling in the pit of his stomach, or Brad was close by, he'd count the days until Thursday.

The park was almost always empty. It was an old, scruffy place. The swings were rusty, so when you sat on them they'd creak with each movement. The slide to the right of the swings was broken, thanks to Brad and his friends. One Friday, Brad stole fireworks from his dad's shed, and he and the band of loyal followers set them off underneath the slide, managing to blow a huge chunk clean off. Ed could recall the moment a police officer escorted Brad up the drive back to his dad after it had happened. Mr Bellua swung open the door and screamed at his sorry-looking son. Ed remembered feeling very angry at the police officer, as he watched him begin to sympathise with Brad and place a protective arm on his shoulder. The officer took both Brad and his dad inside the house. Ed had sat watching the officer closely, stomach churning, thinking "Why are you being so nice to him? He's a monster!"

Back to Thursdays. The one day that kept Ed going from week to week. The one day that, whenever Ed felt like nothing else mattered, made him realise that he had Sam. It was on one particular Thursday evening, though, when Ed's salvation was suddenly ripped right from under his feet, and his world seemed to implode. The friends had raced home to change. Ed reached the meeting point earlier than Sam, so he waited. After a while of patience, he began to wonder if everything was okay. For the first time ever, Sam was late. He waited some more, and then he saw Sam's familiar figure at the end of the road. As Sam grew closer, Ed noticed that his first fear was real. Sam looked like he had been crying. Ed had never seen him cry. The usual happy expression on his best friend's face was gone, and in its place were puffy, red eyes and a glum frown.

"You okay, Sam?" Ed questioned, anxiously.

"Come on, let's get to the park," Sam replied.

Before Ed could ask any more questions, Sam had set off peddling at lightning speed. Ed looked behind to make sure that Brad wasn't on his bike, chasing them. No Brad. So, what was wrong with Sam?

They reached the park, and Sam dumped his bike and raced to the swings, closely followed by his best friend. At this point, there was an ache the size of a fist developing in Ed's stomach. The pair sat swinging in complete silence with only the old, creaky moan from the rusted bars of each swing acting as a welcomed distraction to the quietness between them.

"Sam," Ed said sharply, "Something's up. I'm your best mate, and I think you should tell me. I can hel…". Before he could finish the sentence, Sam blurted out through muffled tears,

"I'm moving!"

"Moving? What do you mean?" Ed asked. He was confused. Surely Sam didn't mean moving house? Or school? What would Ed do without him?

"Dad has a new job in London, so we all have to move there with him. I've got to start a new school and live in a strange city, and I don't want to go, but I sort of have to for Dad," Sam spluttered.

Sam swung his eyes to the ground, tears splashing onto his knees. The boys talked for a short time about what the move would mean, and how it would affect their friendship, but then silence fell again. What had always been Ed's favourite day of the week was now his worst. Thursdays, for Ed, would never be the same again. Ed's incredibly ordinary world was about to become extraordinary, and the lonely boy on the rusty swing had no idea that it was coming.

Chapter 5

Goodbye Sam

As much as Ed loved his family, as every child would understand, there was a special bond between him and his best friend that he couldn't quite explain. It was just there, and, as much as he didn't want to accept that Sam was moving, Ed promised himself that he would make Sam's last couple of weeks the best yet.

They spent every day after school together and, during school, all of their free time in the library working out school holidays and making plans to stay at each other's houses. One evening, while the boys were in the abandoned shed at the bottom of Ed's garden, they created a model of the earth using old clay they had found in a tatty box under a workbench. It took Ed and Sam hours to make it into a perfect sphere shape and then the pair sat on the splintered wooden floor of the shed and used a world atlas to make sure they included every country, continent, and sea.

After the clay had dried, they hunted for tubs of old paint to make it completely realistic and managed to find half a tub of grass green and an unopened container of sky blue. While the world was at their feet, they sat and worked out the distance from Devantrue to London and held a piece of string over the model to demonstrate how short the distance seemed; it was 233 miles and took over four hours to get from start to finish.

The children decided that the best way to keep in touch would be by letter. That way, unlike a simple phone call, a few things would have happened so that every conversation would be interesting. Sam asked his dad for their new address and handed it to Ed on a scrap of paper. Ed stared at the address and promised Sam that he would write first because he knew just how nervous his friend was about starting a new school. But even as he was making this promise, Ed couldn't help but wonder... what would become of him? Who would help him hide from Brad at school? Who would he have to talk to about space and alien life, and whether or not Mrs Hooper at school was, in fact, a Martian?

On the day before Sam was due to leave, he spent his final night at Ed's. Sam's parents still needed to finish packing, so Sam came for tea, too. Games, pizza, and telescope. That night, Ed and Sam looked at the earth model they had made. It was heavy and cold, and as Ed cupped it in the palms of his hands, he could feel the bumps where rolled up pieces of sausage-like clay met to outline all the different countries and oceans. Sam lifted the globe from Ed's grip and rolled the small blue and green weight around in his hands like it was a precious metal. Ed looked on, his fingers smudged with a mixture of clay dust and paint from Australia, which hadn't quite dried properly. Sam spun the globe to show the United Kingdom and placed his index finger somewhere in the middle and his thumb somewhere over London.

"See?" Sam reassured. "When you look at it on here, we're not that far apart at all. You keep the earth model on your window sill, then when you come and visit me in London, I can have a turn of looking after it!"

Ed smiled as Sam got up and placed the model on the window sill, but he didn't reply. On the model, it was only the distance of two fingers, but in reality, 233 miles was a long way, and Sam was the only friend Ed had.

After a restless night trying his best to calm the anxious stormy sea that had erupted in his stomach, Ed woke to the muffled tones of Sam's parents, who had arrived to collect his best friend for the last time. As they were about to leave, Sam gave Ed a hug as his mum said,

"You can come over just as soon as we're settled, Ed; you boys will hardly notice the change when you get used to it."

"Remember the address," Sam whispered as he turned to leave.

Ed stood next to his mum, encased in her right arm while he watched Sam walk to the car. It was packed full of all of their belongings, and he could barely make out Sam's face once he had managed to manoeuvre himself inside the heaving vehicle. Then, as the car pulled away, Ed noticed a small hand waving frantically between a stack of cushions and a suitcase. Ed waved back and smiled, although he couldn't really think of a single reason to. He was alone. Sam was beginning to feel even further away than their mansion on Mars. Ed stood, feeling more alone than ever, with a terrible sinking feeling that recently he had familiarised himself well with. A larger than before double ache had formed once again in the pit of his stomach, and no matter how hard he breathed, it wouldn't disappear. It hurt and ached and niggled away at him from the inside. He couldn't stop it.

Now, before you read any further, remember everything that you have learned about Edward Uset so far. You know all about his mum, his dad and his brother, Jack, everything about Sam, school, and even Bradley Bellua. And for a long time, this was his life. Or at least it was before... well, you should be warned that you're about to read the next part of this story; the part that Ed himself could never have predicted or dreamed of, and one that to this very day, Ed had only ever shared with one very special person. But you have chosen to read this book, so you have chosen to relive a very extraordinary tale. You know all about Ed and how ordinary his life was. Everything you read in the first four chapters was the exact truth, and everything you're about to hear next is just that, the truth. Should you choose to relive the next part of the story, then you need to know that everything that you're going to read happened to Ed over the space of a single day, broken down into six extraordinary moments. And his life changed forever. If you have ever felt like you didn't matter, or that people wouldn't miss you if you were not there, then you will soon learn that every single person on earth has a purpose... this was Ed's.

Chapter 6

Be careful what you wish for...

With Sam gone, the next few days at school were unbearable for Ed. It was almost like Brad knew there was a sadness within Ed, and all he wanted to do was make Ed's life more miserable if that was at all possible. Name-calling, throwing rubbers in lessons, and any attempt at public humiliation; Brad did the lot. Ed attempted to do what his mum had advised and tried to go about his day, keeping himself to himself. He spent any free time in the library, and Thursday nights were now spent at home in the safe enclosure of the den. But even that special place couldn't take away the pain in Ed's stomach. It wasn't a hideout anymore; it was just an empty space. And when he sat in there, alone, all he could think about and feel was the ache in his stomach that was increasing in size at such a rapid pace that it made Ed angry.

As the week passed by, he realised that, actually, without Sam to make school bearable, there wasn't much about his life that he liked at all. It now seemed like a long cycle of the same thing over and over again, counting the days for the weekend when he could be invisible in his room. Then, one miserable Monday, it happened. The thing that you were warned about; that thing that you were told that, up until now, no one has chosen to believe. The next 24 hours were about to change Ed's life forever.

The bell sounded for the end of school, and Ed left, as usual, walking the long way home (the way he knew Brad Bellua and his friends did not go). On the way, he rummaged inside his jacket pockets in the hope of finding some money for a bar of chocolate. An interesting fact about this ache that now held permanent residency in Ed's stomach was that when he ate something deliciously tasty like chocolate, just for a millisecond, the only thing Ed felt was a sweet feeling of fullness and contentment.

As he rummaged and grew closer to the shop, Ed saw two figures in the doorway. Standing right outside, and hovering over two bikes were Brad and Dan. They'd bought sweets, and Brad, whilst clutching a bottle of pop in one hand, was throwing his sweets at Dan's head. Even to his friends, he appeared to be a bully. Ed froze. This was completely unexpected. Standing on the spot, he felt his body grow rigid and stiff as the ache started to wrap itself around his whole stomach. He frantically tried to decide what to do. He couldn't go back, because if he could see them, then they could definitely see him. However, if he raced on, they'd only give chase.

Hoping desperately that Brad was too occupied in his sweet throwing, Ed concluded that today was not a day for chocolate. He carried on silently and began marching in the direction of home. He noticed his shoelace had worked loose but had no time to stop. Clearly, even his walk home from school had now changed; could Brad not even let him have that in peace now? As he marched, he suddenly heard Brad shout,

"Hey Deadward, long time no see!"

So, he had been spotted. He turned his march into a run and then a sprint. The ache in his stomach seemed to be working against him. He felt it pulling him back, and it made him wish that he could suddenly just combust and vanish into thin air. He felt his heavy rucksack weighing him down with every bang of each foot on the hard concrete. If only he could at least make it to Brad's street, he thought. Brad's dad would be sitting on the porch; he would see Brad, yell at him, and, for today, Ed would have escaped. But sure enough, even with Brad biking one-handed whilst clutching his bottle and sweets, he and Dan caught their victim. Brad began edging his bike onto the back of Ed's heels and laughing. His legs felt as heavy as lead; he was slowing down, almost giving up. He didn't know what was worse, his bully trailing hot on his heels or the ache that felt like it had now wrapped itself around every single limb on his body.

"Don't trip, Ed. Hey, why are you running? You're not SCARED, are you?" Brad scoffed.

Brad's bike tyre caught Ed's heel for the fifth time, and he tripped. He bolted his hands outright as his body fell and hit the concrete. As his hands hit the floor, he felt a stinging sensation on his palms that overpowered his feelings of dread and anger. Lying on the ground, all he could do was hope that the fall itself was comedy enough for Brad and that the two of them would bike on. But they didn't, they stopped. Ed clenched his fists and wanted to scream "STOP!"

Brad stood over him as he lay looking down at the fresh grazes on his hands.

"Hey, Dan," Brad smirked. "Let's carry out a little experiment, shall we? I wonder what will happen if I shake this bottle up and then open it over little Deadward here?"

Dan stared at Brad. Ed stared at Dan, who laughed nervously as Brad shook the bottle. Then Brad held it over Ed's head and quickly unscrewed the lid. Ed lay on the ground, being covered in fizzy pop, hands still stinging from the fall.

As he began to force himself up, staying silent, it was clear that Brad and Dan had had their fun. Ed was overcome with rage. He didn't even wait to see if Brad wanted to hurt him again; he simply stood in angry silence. How he hated Brad! Laughing at his expense as he went, Brad jumped on his bike, dropped his bottle to floor, and raced off with Dan swiftly on his tail.

Ed stormed in the direction of home with his mum's voice swirling in his head, telling him what she thought he should do about avoiding Brad at school. It made Ed angry that she only ever seemed to try her hardest to be fair about the whole thing, almost like she felt sorry for Brad for some strange reason. She had even tried telling Ed to speak to Brad, like he had any conscience at all, so really it was entirely Ed's problem and entirely down to him to sort out.

The sodden figure concluded that all he needed to be was more invisible. But how? How can one person like Ed be more invisible than they already were? He avoided Brad at school, he walked a different route home, and he didn't even play out since Sam had left. Maybe, Ed thought, he just needed to BE invisible. That was it. His life would be so much better if he wasn't around. He clenched his fists tight and stretched his torso in a last-ditch attempt to ease his tense stomach. He felt so angry at Brad, and at his mum, and at Sam for leaving. At that very moment, he wished. He wished so hard to be invisible; with eyes squinting, legs shaking, he wished, and then... BANG. Black.

In all the panic of Brad and the sticky pop, which had caused his hair to drape over his eyes, he'd not stopped to tie his lace, and he tripped. For the second time that day he was lying on the floor, but this time, he was alone. He hadn't been as quick to thrust out his hands this time and ended up hitting his head instead. He sat up slowly, head spinning. No blood, just a painful bump. He rubbed it, frustrated.

"I hate my life!" he screamed, as he sat there on the cold path, looking down at the grazes on his hands and the untied lace. He reached up and touched his hair; it was sticky and wet. The only thing Ed felt that he had left was this horrible feeling in his stomach that just wouldn't stop. He squeezed his stomach as tightly as possible in a vice-like grip. No use. Finally, with no other options in his mind, Ed went home to hibernate in the den.

He dumped his sticky uniform in the wash basket, grabbed a plated tea his mum had left in the oven, and went straight to his room. There he hid in the deep, dark enclosure of the den. No console, no snacks, just darkness. He pinned a sign to the bedroom door, which read, 'Do NOT enter, I'm invisible!!!' and then lay in the den, hating life. A short time later, he heard his mum's soft footsteps coming up the stairs. She called out to Ed, but he decided not to answer and instead pretended to be asleep. He could hear a quiet voice reading out the newly pinned sign on the door and then in a faint whisper she said,

"Oh, Ed, I'll be downstairs if you want to talk. Night love."

You may be sitting reading this thinking that the night before the extraordinary 24-hour period was not, in fact, extraordinary at all. But something quite peculiar had already taken place that evening. It may not appear to mean too much to you right now, and it certainly didn't to Ed. But what had happened was set to change the course of history for this young boy in every way imaginable.

Chapter 7

Absent

Ed's alarm buzzed loudly at 7 am the next morning. He sat bolt upright and rubbed the painful lump that had formed on the side of his head, reminding him of what had happened the evening before. He dragged his body from the comfort of the den and looked down at his hands. He blinked several times to clear his eyes, but everything looked warped like he was wearing those 3D glasses you're given in the cinema. He rubbed his eyes with the backs of his hands, shut them tightly, and then opened them wide once again. Still blurred.

"What is this?" he whispered to himself. Beginning to panic, he called his mum,

"Mum, help!" No answer. He tried again, pulling his bedroom door wide open, but nothing. Assuming she had already left for work, Ed was about to race through to Jack's room for advice about his blurred vision when he heard a voice calling him back from inside his room.

"Ed, wait," the voice said.

Ed froze. It was a voice he hadn't heard before. It was calm yet direct, and Ed felt he should do as the voice had said, even though he didn't know its owner. He turned to look back in the direction of the voice. Blinking, his eyes began to focus a little. With every blink he could see that little bit clearer, then, with the final blink, he looked over towards his bed upon which rested a grey, shadowed figure. It looked as though it had been drawn with chalk, shaded in, and smudged slightly with a finger. Ed screamed, but the figure did not move. It remained calm, and when Ed's lungs had no more air left in them, it took its chance to speak again.

"There is no need to be afraid, Ed," it said.

"Please don't hurt me! Y.. you're, you're a...," Ed stuttered, but he couldn't manage to finish his sentence.

The grey figure interrupted, "I'm you, Ed. Well, a part of you anyway. I'm your shadow."

Thinking this was some kind of dream that he hadn't woken up from properly, Ed spun around to look behind him, and sure enough, his shadow was gone. There was just his body, no mirror image of himself that a person would expect to see from the blaze of the morning sun through the window.

"I'm dreaming," Ed told himself.

"No, Ed. You're not dreaming. I am your shadow, and I have been with you for your entire life. I have noticed that, just lately, you haven't been yourself. The wish you made yesterday afternoon; you do remember that, don't you?" the shadow asked.

A frown formed across Ed's face as he scratched his head and began to think. His fingers traced over the painful lump.

"Wish; a wish," Ed muttered. He remembered exactly what he had wished for. He had thought about it more than just yesterday, but he wanted to test the shadow, and the shadow entered willingly into Ed's trap.

"You wished to be invisible, Ed. You clenched your fists, closed your eyes, and then there was the pass-through."

"Wait," snapped Ed. "The pass-through? What does that even mean?"

The shadow continued, "The pass-through is when a collision happens — an event; something big enough to transport a person between two realms. You wished with every inch of your body; you wished so hard that your wish passed through your body and into me, your shadow, and then you fell. This was where the pass-through occurred. Your event was the bang of your head. The collision between you and the ground combined by the power of the wish transported you straight from the ordinary realm to the realm of invisibility and, well, here we are now."

"Wait," responded Ed. "You cannot actually expect me to believe that a shadow sitting on the end of my bed claiming to belong to me and...," Ed paused, turning his head from side to side to check that he hadn't missed his shadow "...telling me that I've moved into a whole other realm is real? If it's real, then why am I still in my room? In my house? How do you explain that?"

"Eyes blurred when you woke up? Looks almost like you're inside a telescope, doesn't it? Everything isn't quite the same; distorted you might say. You don't get that in the ordinary realm, Ed. Go outside this room and call for Jack, and I can guarantee he won't hear you. You could wave and jump in his face, and he wouldn't see a thing," Ed's shadow explained.

Ed's eyes began to widen. He started blinking again and scanning the room, then paused,

"Wait, you said Jack. That's my brother."

"Yes, your brother. Ed, I have been with you from the minute you were born. I was there when you and Sam got stuck up that oak tree for three hours waiting for Dad to save us; I was there when you fell over in nursery and had to have stitches, and I was there when Dad took you to get your first telescope. I know everything about you; I am part of you," the shadow explained.

"Then why are you not with me now?" Ed quizzed.

"A shadow is not needed in the realm of invisibility. What invisible person do you know who would need a shadow?" Ed was deep in thought at the shadow's response. "Look down to your waist," it continued. Ed followed the instruction and glanced down. His eyes stopped upon a hologram belt that was wrapped around his waist. It was black and metal looking, and across the front there were six round, golden circles. He went to touch it, but his hand went straight through. "You can't control the tokens, Ed; many have tried, but that is out of your power."

"Wait, what? What is this thing? What are tokens? I don't understand," Ed felt a surge of panic and straightened up in anticipation of the familiar ache beginning its journey around his stomach.

"Ed, you are invisible. You are now living in the realm of invisibility. No one in the ordinary realm can see or hear you, and you cannot affect anything in the ordinary realm freely. You have, around your waist, six tokens. Each token permits you to alter or make one thing happen in the ordinary realm; you can spend them one at a time."

Ed's shadow paused and stood up, moving silently towards Ed. Ed stepped back. His mind raced at the possibilities of what he was hearing. If this was true, then he now had everything he wanted. He could spend all of the tokens on punishing Brad.

"Ed," the shadow continued, with a serious tone. "You need to listen to what I am about to say very carefully. The tokens are not limitless; they do not replenish. You have six and six only. When your final token is spent, you will remain in the realm of invisibility without the power to ever affect the ordinary realm again. You will only exist; watching your old life continue without you. Do you understand?"

Ed looked deep into the murky grey of his shadow, "Yes, I understand. I get these tokens; I can make things happen, but once they are gone, that's it."

"Then you are ready," the shadow finished.

"Ready?" Ed asked. "Ready for what? What happens now?"

"You are ready for your six extraordinary moments. Each token you spend will be a moment that will alter your thinking. Only you can decide how you spend them. You need to go about your journey alone in order to decide what happens next." The shadow began to move away towards the galaxy printed wall in Ed's room.

"Wait! No, stay. I need you. How do I know what to do or where to go? You can't leave me!" Ed shouted.

The shadow paused in its movement and turned. "I will appear when I am needed, and a token I will take, be careful what you wish for, boy with the ache." Then it disappeared into the speckled galaxy wall.

Ed stood for a moment and then looked back down at the belt. Each of the six tokens shone and glistened as they caught the light. They felt precious and had given Ed a sudden surge of comfort. He began to feel happiness, a warm blanket smothering his body. He hadn't felt that for a long time. With no time to waste in this new state of invisibility, Ed began to move. He knew exactly where he would start and how to use his first token. He would go to school to find the one person who had made his life more miserable than he could ever have imagined. It was time, Ed thought, for revenge.

In all the excitement of the belt and tokens, it had slipped Ed's mind that it was now very close to school time and, being unable to be seen or heard in the ordinary realm, his absence was about to be noted for the first time that day.

Ed had never raced to school so quickly. He finally arrived, sprinted up the cobbled path that seemed oddly smooth and cushioned in this realm, and headed straight for his classroom. The children had already piled in and were beginning to seat themselves at their desks. He scanned the room and spotted Brad, being spoken to sternly by Mr Dion. The teacher called for everyone to be quiet, and with that, a silence fell over the room. Ed stood at the back of the room, trying to stay silent. He had somehow forgotten that he could no longer be seen or heard. He could feel his heart beating in his ears. Mr Dion started the register. Name after name was called, and a resounding, "Yes, Sir" could be heard in chorus after each one. Finally, at the very end of the register, he called Ed's name. No answer came after the first call, so Mr Dion tried again, not lifting his head from the file of endless ticks. He paused, placed his finger on Ed's name, and looked up towards Ed's usual seat.

"Ed not here today? Does anyone know if he's ill? Has anyone seen him this morning?" Mr Dion called to the class.

"I think, Sir," Brad interrupted, "that little Deadward is at home drying off." Brad turned to look at Dan to receive a laugh from their private joke.

"Bradley Bellua, you are on your second warning this morning already, and it's only ten past nine. One more warning and you'll get lunchtime detention," Mr Dion barked. Brad rolled his eyes and looked down at his desk, maintaining his usual angry expression. Mr Dion scribbled something down on a blank piece of paper on his desk and sent Peter Tapper with the note to the office.

"Right, everyone remain seated. Mrs Hooper will be in shortly to take science, and I will be back straight after break time. I expect everyone to be on their best behaviour." Mr Dion glared at Brad as Mrs Hooper burst into the room.

Chapter 8

The Revenge Moment

Ed had spent years being terrified of Brad and trying to avoid him and his friends. Now, with every inch of his body tingling at the thought of his newly devised plan, he decided that revenge was a dish best served cold... and wet. As he stood at the back of the classroom with his eyes fixed on the back of Brad's head, Mrs Hooper instructed several pupils to hand out one measuring jug of blue liquid and one bottle of clear liquid to every child. When everyone had their equipment, Ed stared down at the belt with the golden tokens.

"How do I use one of these things?" he whispered to himself, attempting to grab one.

"So, you're ready for your first moment?" Ed jumped and spun around. His shadow had returned, which meant that Ed needed him.

"Yes," replied Ed. "I know how I want to use my first token. I want to humiliate Brad in front of everyone. That's my first moment," Ed said, confidently.

"And you're sure this is it? You want to spend one of your six tokens on this?" His shadow looked at him, intently.

"Why does it sound like you're judging me? If you've been with me forever, then you should know what he has done to me!" Ed said in a frustrated manner, as he pointed a finger towards Brad.

The shadow spoke once more, "I'm not judging you, Ed, I'm simply ensuring that you are sure. You only have six moments, and once they are gone, there is no going back. If this is what you want for your first moment, then a token will be taken from your belt and what you wish for will become a reality."

"I wish for Brad to be humiliated just like I have been because of him," Ed said.

With that, there was a clatter. A panic erupted through the class; some shouts, some laughs, and a resounding yell from Mrs Hooper. Brad was covered in the liquid from the bottle on his desk; his chair had tipped causing him to fall backwards, he had hit the table behind and was soaked for the second time in Peter Tapper's bottle of solution.

"Bradley Bellua, get out of this room immediately! All you seem to do is cause destruction wherever you go," Mrs Hooper barked.

With that, Brad launched to his feet and stormed out of the room with the door swinging behind him. Ed looked down at the belt. A single token began to lose its gleam and slowly fade away, as did his shadow.

"Peter, please can you go and get some paper towels from the toilet?" Mrs Hooper yelled. Peter stood obediently and began to leave the room, followed closely by Invisible Ed.

Ed reached the corridor and looked to his left where rows of bags and jumpers were hung from pegs and, amid the hanging objects, sat Brad. He was dripping wet. Ed moved closer and stood over him just as Brad had stood over Ed on the evening at the shop. Ed watched as the sullen boy on the floor wiped tears from his face and solution from his trousers. He, Ed, had done that. Suddenly, the anchored ache in the pit of his stomach pulled again slightly. He couldn't quite work out if he was pleased that he had got

Brad back, or disappointed in himself that he had, in fact, acted just like the one person he hated the most. Ed knew all too well how it felt to be embarrassed in front of his class. Was that the reason the ache tugged inside of him? He didn't give himself time to dwell, he'd had his first moment, and it was what he had deserved for so long.

Chapter 9

Meeting Maggie Bas

The bell for break time rang through the school, which swiftly emptied as everyone scrambled outside to play. After all the excitement of Brad and the revenge, Ed decided that to ease the ache that he had been left with, he'd visit the library. It was quiet and peaceful but wasn't quite the same without Sam. As he wandered through his familiar silent sanctuary, Ed spotted a girl that he hadn't noticed before. She had long, dark, curly hair and a lonely look on her face as she sat by herself fingering the pages of a large book. The only thing that seemed cheery about this girl was the silky, floppy blue and black bow that was pinned to the side of her hair. Ed moved closer as she closed the book she had been browsing. It was entitled 'Space – Another World'. Anyone who liked space was okay with Ed, so he edged closer still, catching sight of one of the lonely girl's school books. It was labelled Maggie Bas.

Ed sat beside Maggie for a while. He thought she was interesting, but no one seemed to notice her. No one came to sit with her, and it didn't look like she was waiting for anyone; she was just reading. Every now and again she would pause and place a scruffy looking leather bookmark under the word she had got to, lift her head and quickly scan the room as though she was hoping for someone, anyone, to notice her. But nobody did.

The bell for the end of break time sounded, and she silently gathered up her things to leave. Ed followed as though the pair were friends walking to class together. Maggie meandered quietly through school. She was pushed and shoved in the crowds of people all busy making their way to class, but she didn't react once. After observing the mysteriously unknown character for a while, Ed began to realise that maybe not everyone needed to make a wish to be invisible.

Maggie had sent Ed into a universe of wonder. He'd never noticed her before, but she clearly knew the library well.

"I need to do something," he said aloud, waiting in anticipation for the shadow to reappear. Sure enough, it arrived.

"So," it said, standing beside Ed. "This is your second moment? You've never noticed Maggie before, but she has been here, in the same place each day. We've often walked past her," said Ed's shadow.

"But if I've walked past her before, I surely would have seen her?" Ed looked confused.

"Maybe you were looking but not seeing. There was more in the ordinary realm than you gave time to, Ed. Much more," the shadow explained.

"Well, I'd like to make Maggie feel noticed. I'd like her to feel like she matters. I get how that feels. I felt like that," Ed said.

"A wise moment. Consider it done," the shadow whispered.

With that, the second token on Ed's belt began to fade. The shadow vanished, and Ed watched Maggie sitting in class as he tried to anticipate what might unfold next. Then there was a knock on the classroom door.

"Come in," the teacher called at the front of the class. A student entered the room holding a book. It read 'Mysteries of Outer Space' on the cover; one of Ed's favourite books. Poking just out of the top was a thin slip of paper. The student approached the teacher and held out the book.

"This has been left in the library for Maggie Bas," the student explained. The teacher took the book and walked over to Maggie. She looked surprised, taken aback that someone even knew her name, let alone had given her something.

"Maggie, there you are dear," the teacher whispered, and she placed the book on the edge of Maggie's desk. A low murmur began to hum across the class from the disturbance of the deliverer.

"Shhhh! Quiet please and continue with your writing, we have fifteen minutes before we stop for lunch," the teacher ordered.

Maggie stayed silent and secretly reached out to examine the book. She read the title and then opened the book to reveal the note. Ed moved closer, so he was able to read it too.

Dear Maggie,
A gift from one space fan to another, I hope you like it!

A wide grin began to spread from one side of Maggie's face to the other. Happiness radiated out of her like a sunbeam, and she scanned the room to see if anyone was looking in on her private moment of joy. But no one was.

Ed left the classroom and Maggie, and started walking. He wasn't quite sure where to, but he felt that there were no more moments to be had at school. He moved through the building and into the office then out towards the entrance. On this ordinary route, he spotted an entirely unusual figure. A tall man in a fluorescent uniform jacket was grasping a notepad in his right hand. Ed recognised the figure. It was the police officer that had taken Brad home the time he had destroyed the slide at the park. Ed's mind began to wonder, why was the police officer at school? What was he going to the office for? Surely you can't arrest a child? But there was no time to stand and dwell, and with Maggie on his mind, he left school behind and headed into town. Maybe there was a moment to be had there, he thought.

Chapter 10

Revenge Moment II

The centre of town was empty. So, this is what town is like during school time, Ed thought to himself. A few strangers wandered past him, in no rush at all. They all appeared relaxed like they didn't have a care in the world. Since Ed was invisible, he wondered if this was how he should feel now, no concerns or worries. However, something wasn't quite right. Just then, he noticed one lonely figure that was very familiar to him; his dad. Ed's heart sank, and the ache pulled at his stomach. A sudden surge of emotion ran through Ed's body all the way down to his toes.

"No, stop it. You've only been gone for a morning, no going back," Ed muttered to himself, as his eyes fixed on his dad leaving a sandwich shop with his hands full.

"I sensed seeing Dad would make you feel like this," a voice spoke. Ed spun around to see that the loyal shadow had reappeared.

"I don't need you; this isn't a moment," snapped Ed, trying his best not to cry. "I don't miss my family; I love this realm." He attempted to convince the shadow and himself, but even he knew it wasn't true.

Ed followed in pursuit of his dad with the shadow close behind him. His dad led the pair back to his place of work. Ed watched as his dad took a deep breath and opened the door to the building. He followed. Once inside a deep, bellowing voice echoed through the entrance. "About time, I need you to take a shorter lunch today. We have two new orders, and I want them sorted before you leave tonight."

The owner of the voice appeared - a small, chubby man with wiry grey hair and crumbs down his t-shirt that was in fact far too tight to fit his huge stomach. He wore an angry frown on his face and his chunky sausage like fingers were clenched into fists. To Ed, this man and his expressions weren't all that unfamiliar. It was a grown-up Brad.

Ed didn't like how the man spoke to his dad. There was no please, no thank you, and no polite tone. Order after order was barked straight in his dad's face.

"Bullies aren't nice," Ed said, menacingly. He had heard enough. "This; this is my next moment," he asserted.

The shadow heard its prompt and moved next to Ed.

"And what moment is it that you are wanting to change, Ed?" his shadow asked.

"Revenge," answered Ed. "I want this man to feel the way that he makes my dad feel. I want him to feel the way Brad makes me feel."

"And you're sure?" asked his shadow.

"Yes, certain," insisted Ed.

He glanced down at the belt around his waist, and sure enough, just like the previous times, a single token began to lose its glisten and slowly disappear, taking the shadow with it. Then the strangest thing happened. Five individual sachets of salt that lay next to a giant mug of steaming hot black coffee and a plate filled with beans, sausages, eggs, and buttered toast, began floating up into the air. The tops tore off and fell to the desk. The sachets floated over the plate and then hung directly over the mug of coffee. Ed stood, smiling in anticipation. The sachets tilted and the salt poured straight into the mug and disappeared into the black mass of liquid. Not noticing the magic that had just taken place, the bossy giant slumped over to a scruffy looking leather chair, picked up a sausage and devoured it in two single bites, lifted the steaming mug, and began to gulp. He slurped away, washing the sausage down with his salty coffee. Then he stopped. Mouth bursting with liquid, his nose scrunched up to his eyes and his lips began to purse. And then, just as his face began to turn so red that Ed thought the giant may just burst, coffee sprayed out of his mouth, all over the desk and plate of food, as the man uttered disgusted 'urgh' and 'yak' noises. Ed was pleased. So wrapped up was Ed in this sweet revenge that he didn't notice his dad run out of the building in a panic with his phone clutched in his hand. Nor did his dad's boss for that matter.

"Only three moments left," Ed said to himself.

It was mid-afternoon, and Ed was standing outside his dad's work, wondering what to do next. The moments that he'd experienced so far were going to be hard to top, but now that he had got his revenge, and helped Maggie, he wondered what other moments there could possibly be. He didn't want to go home just yet, so he wandered up to a nearby wall to make his next plan.

Ed watched as his legs swung below and people walked past entirely unaware that he was there. It was a strange feeling. Just at that moment, he spotted a street sign with labels on it: library, tourist information centre, cinema. The cinema! One of his favourite places to go with Sam. It was a place a lot like the den for Ed, just bigger.

For weeks he had been begging his parents to take him to watch the new space movie, The Lost Astronaut. Both his mum and dad had promised him, on more than one occasion, that they would make time to take him but never had. Well, Ed thought, if they didn't have time to take him, then he would go himself. After all, he didn't need an adult to accompany him or money for a ticket. If no one could see him, then he could sneak in and watch the film completely unnoticed.

He walked up to the cinema doors and slipped through. It was relatively empty, just a few people scattered around. He stopped in front of the pick 'n' mix stand, wondering whether to spend one of his tokens on sweets, but thought better of it when he looked at his belt and saw only three left shining. Resisting temptation, he walked across to look at the film times. The Lost Astronaut - next showing - 13:00. He glanced at the clock; it was twenty minutes to one, perfect! He walked through to screen six and found a seat right on the very top tier at the back. No teachers, no lessons, no Brad; Ed couldn't quite believe just how lucky he was in that moment. The film was just as good as he had expected it to be, but as he left the dark room and the light hit his eyes, he stood feeling a little empty. As lucky as he was to be at the cinema on a school day, he had no one to tell. No one to share it with.

As he stepped out into the fresh air, he saw people from school. It was three thirty. Just then, and unusually on his own, he spotted another figure he knew all too well; his big brother, Jack. He appeared to be going in every single shop, only for a few minutes, and then coming back out again. What was he doing? Why was he on his own? Ed decided to investigate.

Chapter 11

The temporary doubt

In all the excitement of the revenge, the cinema, and meeting Maggie, it hadn't occurred to Ed that the note Mr Dion had sent to the office earlier that morning was, in fact, about him. If a child doesn't attend school, then parents are rung. In Ed's case, his parents were not able to tell the school that he was off with a sickness, or maybe running a fever. They didn't know where Ed was, nobody did. Ed was missing.

As Ed had left school that morning, he had passed a police officer and, unbeknownst to Ed, all of these events were about to make sense.

Outside the shops in town, he caught up with his brother and trailed after Jack as he entered the next shop. It was a small bakery that was run by an old lady called Mrs Broach, who had been a friend of the family since Ed was a baby. A small woman with soft grey hair who always wore a woolly cardigan, no matter the weather. She had often looked after Ed and Jack when they were younger, and whenever she did, she would always bring the most delicious homemade cakes for them both. She was patient and kind, and they liked her.

Jack walked up to the glass counter; Ed close behind. Ed watched his older brother waiting to get Mrs Broach's attention. Half his concentration was on his brother, the other half on the multi-coloured array of cakes, flapjacks, macaroons, and biscuits that stood in uniform behind a pane of cold glass. The oven in the back room was fired up and oozing the sweetest scent of toffee from its doors. Ed loved this shop.

"Hi, Jack, how are you holding up, sweetie?" Mrs

Broach asked in a gentle voice.

"Not great," Jack replied. "We've got some flyers made up; I wondered if you would mind putting some up in the window and maybe leaving some on the counter? We want everyone to be aware in case anyone has seen him."

Mrs Broach gave a supportive smile. "Of course I will, Jack. And don't you worry. I've known you and Eddy a very long time, and I know that both of you are very smart and lovely young men. He has an amazing life ahead of him, and he will make a grand scientist one day. You mark my words; he'll be back."

Ed stepped back. He had caught sight of the posters that Jack was holding. They displayed his face, a number, and at the top, 'MISSING' in bold letters. He let out a single gasp.

"Surely you knew this would happen, Ed?" The familiar voice of the shadow had returned, but this time Ed didn't turn to look in its direction. Instead, he stood gaping at the two people he knew so well talking about him. "You may not think so, but Jack and your mum and dad love you, unconditionally. Families are busy, but that doesn't take away from how they feel. Unconditional love means it can never go away, never stop," the shadow explained.

"What's happening?" Ed questioned, in a panicked tone.

"This morning, Jack waited for you to walk you to school, but obviously, he couldn't see you. Then Mr Dion informed your parents that you hadn't turned up to class. The police officer you passed as you left school arrived because your mum had contacted them. While you were watching your third moment, your dad ran from work and set off for home. That was because of you, Ed. You didn't think you could simply transport from the ordinary realm without consequence, did you? The fact is, you cannot be in both realms at the same time. In the ordinary realm, you are a missing person," the shadow warned gravely. Ed stood in silence.

He watched on as Mrs Broach spoke, confident that he would come back, like she knew he wasn't in any danger. Jack appeared to look reassured by Mrs Broach's words.

"Now then, you've handed out lots of these leaflets, the police are out there with your mum and dad looking, so there's no point in you making yourself ill now, is there? They have enough to worry about. Stop a few minutes and have a drink and some cake, won't you?" Mrs Broach asked.

"But we need to keep looking," Jack argued. Mrs Broach gave a sympathetic smile, walked from behind the counter, and wrapped her arms around Jack.

"Five minutes, just to get your energy back, and then you can go back out there and carry on," she said, decisively. They walked to a small table in the back room, and she started plating up slices of cake and making Jack a drink. Ed peered through at his brother; he was sitting with his head in his hands.

Worried, and with the tension growing more prominent in his stomach, Ed felt like he had only one option left, to go home. He walked home with his head bowed and questions racing through his mind. So many he couldn't keep up.

Back home, he walked through the door and, unusually, both his mum and dad were home. His mum was pacing up and down the kitchen like a caged lion, while his dad spoke on the phone. He ended the conversation and placed the phone down on the side.

"The police officer we saw to this morning is coming round again. Half the neighbourhood is out looking; we will get him home," his dad reassured. Ed walked over to a chair, sat down with his legs heavy, and watched as his parents panicked.

A few minutes later, a loud and formal knock at the door made Ed jump as he sat at the kitchen table, staring at Mum, Dad, and Jack, who had just arrived back home. They all looked very anxious. His dad stood up, took a deep breath, and walked towards the door. A tall, stocky man with a neon vest and radios strapped to him bowed his head under the door frame and walked right into the kitchen. He had a sympathetic smile on his face, and he shook Mr Uset's hand as Ed's dad led him to the table at which the whole family sat.

Ed was paralysed by the tense ache in his stomach. He didn't know what to do and felt almost as if he was intruding on a meeting he shouldn't be at. He found the strength to drag his limp body up and edge backwards into a corner of the kitchen, out of the way of the group. The officer sat down next to his Mum, reached up to his giant head, and lifted off his black velvet looking hat that had a shining silver badge pinned to the front. He pulled out a small notepad, the kind that a waiter brings to the table when they take your food at a restaurant. Wait, thought Ed; he recognised the officer. He stared at him, trying to figure out where he'd seen him before. School! This was the officer that Ed passed on the way out of school, the same officer that was with Brad when he took Brad home after the incident at the park. When this officer was with Brad, it was because he had done something wrong. Is this the officer they send to kids who are like Brad? Kids who do bad things? Ed panicked.

"I'm PC Pritchett, but you can call me Mark," the fluorescent giant introduced himself. "I'm sorry that this meeting isn't under better circumstances, but I want to assure you we're working as hard as we can to find Edward as soon as possible," he explained.

Ed's mum wiped tears from her eyes and then turned her head towards the officer,

"PC Pritchett, erm, Mark, I don't know why Ed would want to, to…" she paused and sobbed, tears falling from her eyes on to the table like huge raindrops. His dad pulled his chair up and put his arm around her.

"I think what my wife is trying to say, is that this is just not like Ed. He's a good kid. I mean, yes, we're all busy, but we get by, and he's never said anything about wanting to run away. Nothing. We're a normal family." Ed's dad appeared to grow frustrated, and he put his head in his hands. Jack sat still, looking down at the table.

PC Pritchett interrupted, "I can see that you are a great family, there is no doubting that. Look, there could be a whole list of reasons why Ed has decided to leave home, and not a single one of them may even be related to home. So please, don't beat yourselves up. You guys need to pull together so that when we bring Ed home, you're the best support system for him."

This police officer, Mark, seemed like quite a nice man to Ed. He wasn't blaming him or his mum or dad. He was trying to help, his voice was soft and calm, and it made Ed's heart slow down to a steadier beat.

"I understand you have friends and family out looking, and we've given a description to our team about your son, but I need to ask a few more questions about Ed so that we have a good picture of how he may have been feeling before he left. We also need to gain more of an idea of his interests, friends, and where he might go for help," Mark explained.

"He was fine before he left. He always just gets on with things, we never hear a peep from him," his dad reassured.

"No," mum interrupted. "Sam. Sam's moved." Ed's dad looked at his mum and then at Jack. He looked shocked like he didn't know. Mum continued, looking at Mark, "Sam is Ed's best friend, well I think his only friend. They did everything together. I met Sam's mum years ago, and the boys hit it off. They've been in the same class since nursery school. A few weeks ago, Sam's mum called me to tell me they were moving to London; her husband has a promotion at work." As mum spoke, Mark was frantically jotting down words in his notebook and flipping page after page as he wrote. Ed never knew there were this many details about his life.

"Did Ed know that Sam was leaving?" Mark questioned.

"Yes, he knew, we waved Sam off just the other

week. When Sam's mum first phoned, I said I'd sit Ed down and chat to him, but Sam wanted to tell Ed himself. I was going to let Sam and Ed talk it through, and then I was going to have a night with Ed, just me and him. You know, where we both sat down, talked and worked through it, but I just haven't found the time these past few days. Work has been… oh no, it's my fault. I should have talked to him about Sam going!" Mum began crying again.

With this, Jack finally looked up from the table.

"Ed doesn't get on with Brad, the kid who lives across the street."

"Ahh, Bradley Bellua?" Mark asked.

"Yeah, that's him. Ed's always saying that Brad is doing stuff to him. That's why I walk him to school in the morning, so Brad doesn't give him any hassle. But I don't think he's all that keen on school. I guess now Sam's left he doesn't have any mates." Jack looked guilty, obviously blaming himself.

Ed didn't know what to do or think. He hadn't realised that disappearing would cause all of this upset.

"It's no one's fault," Mark said in a reassuring tone. "We have Ed's school details, and I'm having another meeting there tomorrow. I can chat with Brad and a few of the kids at school, and I'll contact Sam's mum down in London. I understand this must be hard for everyone, but we have a few more things to go on now. You mentioned on the phone earlier that Ed likes the park and the cinema in town. We have officers out looking as we speak. The best thing you guys can do is be there for each other and get some rest if you can. Someone should wait here in case Ed comes home. We'll send a family liaison officer to stay with you. My sergeant mentioned the photos on the phone too, do you have those for me to take?"

Ed's mum stood up and went to the kitchen drawer. She pulled out a small pile of photographs and passed them to Mark. He took hold of them and looked down at Ed's face and smiled. He reached out one of his large hands to Ed's parents.

"We'll find him," he promised, as he shook three trembling hands. Little did Mark know, thought Ed, that was one promise only Ed knew he couldn't keep.

Ed watched through the kitchen window as Mark left, and he felt a sudden surge of guilt run through his body. Would their feelings of worry and loss last forever? Would Mum stop crying eventually? As he sat watching and asking himself questions he couldn't find the answers to, he spotted Brad walking with his head down. He remembered that he had got Brad back for everything he had had to put up with over the years. He had punished his dad's horrid boss and managed to go a whole day without being hit, shoved, laughed at, or having to hide at school. For the first time, it wasn't him who was hurt or embarrassed. The ache began to ease just a little.

"Mum and Dad have Jack. This will all calm down, and they can get back to their busy lives in no time, they don't need me. Besides, what can I do anyway? No one can see me. I still have three moments left; I can't stop now," Ed convinced himself. Suddenly, the shadow appeared.

"It's time," it spoke without warning, "that you see how your moments have impacted the ordinary realm, Ed. You should follow Brad. I think you need to see more of what you haven't seen in the ordinary realm."

Just as soon as the shadow arrived, it left again, leaving Ed curious as to what it meant. In the hope of discovering the meaning of the shadow's riddle, Ed set off towards the Bellua house.

Chapter 12

The Empty Room

Ed caught up to Brad just as he reached the rusty green gate which lead up to his house. Ed looked on as Brad met his dad, who was sitting on the porch clasping his usual aluminium cans.

"Bradley, you get here now! Don't think I don't know what you're holding; I've just had that teacher of yours on the phone again. Another science lesson you've been kicked out of!" Brad skulked over to his dad obediently, holding what was evidently a detention slip.

"I've had enough of this, Bradley. You know I'm trying to get a new job sorted, the last thing I need is you and that school of yours giving me more grief!"

As his dad bellowed at him, Brad tried to answer, "But Dad, today I…" His dad held up his hand and silenced Brad.

"I don't want to hear it, Bradley; you need to be a little less YOU in school and a little more invisible. I don't know what time you call this. I'm off to clear my head; sort yourself some tea and if you didn't already know, your computer is gone for the rest of the week."

Brad's dad left the porch and marched down the street, leaving Brad alone with Ed. He stormed into the house, Ed in hot pursuit, and slammed the door behind them. In that moment, Ed started to understand a little why Brad was always so angry, and this time, it was Ed who had made coming home ten times worse for Brad than it already was.

Ed had no idea that Brad had to look after himself at home. Ed's parents worked a lot, but he always had Jack, and there would always be tea left in the oven when his mum wasn't home. His first revenge moment didn't seem as much fun as it had done earlier that day. Ed almost felt uncomfortable walking away, like he was responsible for

Brad. He started remembering the times that his mum had told him to try speaking to Brad on his own about how he felt. Maybe she knew about Brad's dad.

The Bellua house was dark and gloomy looking. There were no photographs on the walls, and all the curtains were drawn. Brad began stomping upstairs and, unable to keep up, Ed heard a door slam and the dull echo of sobs. He followed the muffled sound until he found himself standing directly outside a chipped, dented old bedroom door. There was a sign in the middle hung up by a single rusty nail that read 'KEEP OUT'. Ed was sure he had found Brad's room. He pushed the door with a single finger, and it edged open, creaking slightly. Ed breathed in and snuck through the narrow gap to discover Brad curled up in a ball on his bare bedroom floor. It didn't look like somebody's room. It was empty apart from a single bed and one set of brown drawers that had a foot missing, so they had to lean on the wall to stay upright. There was no paint on the walls, and definitely no handmade bed with a built-in den like Ed's.

The aching feeling Ed was now so used to having made another appearance. It bolted through his stomach, and he knew the reason. He missed home, his mum and his dad, his room and, after seeing how lonely Brad looked there on the floor, he missed Jack.

Ed perched on the edge of the messy, unmade bed in Brad's cold room and watched someone who he had never realised was this vulnerable. Next to him was a pile of papers. They had drawings and scribbles all over them. Ed tilted his head to read the writing and saw the word 'ANGRY' which had been written all over the page on top of the pile. In between the words were pictures of faces that looked a lot like Brad's. Some were crying, and others looked mad. He glanced at Brad. He seemed so frustrated and sad all at the same time. In that moment, Ed wanted to speak to him, to tell him he understood how he was feeling, and that he wasn't on his own.

The shadow appeared and stood still next to the crying boy on the floor.

"Everything okay, Ed?" it asked.

"No," Ed replied, honestly. "I don't like Brad, but I don't want to see another person this upset. I only meant the first moment to embarrass Brad in front of the class, to get him back. I didn't want this; I'm not a bad person."

"No, Ed, you're not a bad person," his shadow replied. "I'm here because I sensed that you are ready to use your next token. Is this a moment you'd like to change?"

"I want to use a token, but I don't want to use it here. It has to involve school. I can't help Brad here. But I know someone who can," Ed said.

"Say no more." The shadow bent down next to Brad and stole a single blank piece of paper from Brad's pile. With that, it left the two boys in the room.

"Wait!" called Ed. "What's the moment? How do you know who the someone is? I haven't told you, wait!" But the shadow had gone, and so had his fourth token.

"Only two left," Ed sighed.

Chapter 13

Homesick

CURRENCY OF

The Realm of Invisibility

THIS COIN PERMITS THE USE OF ONE MAGIC MOMENT. PLEASE USE WITH CAUTION

As Ed left the Bellua house, wondering how the shadow had known what his fourth moment was, a sheet of newspaper came hurling past him and blew into a nearby lamp post. Ed approached the lamp post and scanned the creased paper.

Advert - WANTED:
Qualified joiner to be a part of our up and coming,
friendly team of designers in creating new
and bespoke furniture.

Without hesitation, Ed called for his shadow.

"Shadow! Shadow, I need you!" Sure enough, the shadow appeared next to the lamp post, leaning against the post looking towards the paper.

"Ed, you only have two tokens left. Are you sure this is a moment? I have only just finished completing your last one," the shadow said.

"This has to be a moment," replied Ed. "My dad has always been there for me; I want to give him this."

Full of concern over whether or not the shadow had understood his last moment properly, Ed began to explain his idea.

"This next token has to be used for my dad. This advert for the job, I need you to get it to my dad somehow so that he can go for an interview. His boss doesn't deserve him."

"If this is how you want to spend your fifth token, then, of course, I will make it happen as you wish. But remember, there will only be one token left before you will remain in the realm of invisibility without any power until the end of time. Go forward with caution," his shadow warned. It disappeared, taking another token with it.

Feeling homesick, Ed left for home. He walked in through the front door and began searching the house. No Mum or Dad, but to his surprise, hidden away in Ed's very room, Jack sat on the end of the bed. He was sat holding a CD that Ed always wanted to borrow but was never allowed to, and he was crying. Ed stared at Jack. He had realised today, more than ever, just how much his brother cared for him. The shadow was right; this was what it had called unconditional love.

Ed walked over to the bed and sat next to Jack.

"You'll be okay, Jack," Ed said. "You have Mum and Dad, and all of your friends. You are everything I wanted to be."

Ed sat for a while and looked around the room. It had always been so homely to Ed, but for the first time, it felt different. Empty maybe. After a while, the front door opened. Jack bolted up, wiped the tears from his eyes and turned and placed the CD on Ed's pillow.

"Miss you mate, even if you are my annoying little brother," Jack sniffed to himself. Then he left Ed on the bed, alone again.

Ed didn't want to be alone. He had gone almost a whole day with nobody but his own shadow to talk to. The revenge had filled Ed with what he felt was a short-lived joy. He was surprised that becoming invisible hadn't made the ache disappear at all. In fact, it was with him more in this realm than it had been in the ordinary realm. Wanting to quiet his own thoughts, he ventured downstairs to find it was his mum who had come in through the door. She was on the phone to the police officer again, and she was upset.

Ed stood with just a single token left on the hologram

belt. It seemed to glow a little less than the rest had done, and his vision was beginning to blur like he was wearing the 3D glasses again. He wanted to hug his mum, he wanted to tell his dad about his day, he wanted to let Jack know that to him, Jack was his hero. He felt tears filling up his eyes. He looked down as they fell and disappeared into nothing before they had even touched the floor.

"Shadow, I need you," he sobbed. His shadow walked in through the kitchen door but didn't say a single word. Instead, he walked past Ed and beckoned him through the hallway and up the stairs. Ed obediently followed. The two unlikely friends journeyed into Ed's room, and Ed crawled after the grey figure as it went into the den.

"What's on your mind, Ed?" it asked.

"I don't like this. This realm. I thought I wanted this; I thought I wanted to be invisible, but it isn't what I thought it would be. You were right; I was looking without seeing. But now, I don't know what I should do to use this last moment, because there is nothing I can think of that I want to change. I just wish none of this had happened. I wish I hadn't wished so hard," Ed cried.

"You have created five very different moments, Ed. Some you have learnt from; some you have used to cause others to see differently. Your time in this realm hasn't been wasted, but now you need to think. Is being invisible truly what you want forever?" the shadow questioned.

"No," replied Ed. "But now I'm here, and my family are there, and I can't take it all back." Ed signed and held his head in his hands.

"Ed," comforted his shadow. "You must never want to change what has already been. These things were moments that have changed you. When I came to you this morning and welcomed you into this realm, you were pleased. If it wasn't for your five moments today, I fear that you would still wish to be invisible. This isn't the end, Ed. You still have the sixth token left. I told you to use them wisely, and this final token should be used with the greatest caution of all."

"You can take it," Ed sobbed, as he looked down at the single token. "All I want is to go home; there is nothing else I would use it for."

"Well, if that is definitely what you wish, then consider it done," replied the shadow.

It vanished from the den taking with it the final token and the hologram belt that hovered around Ed's waist. Confused, Ed yawned through tears that ran from his eyes. He was exhausted. Crawling out from the lonely den, he carried himself to the bed and nestled down on top of his duvet.

"Shadow," he yawned, "please don't leave me."

Before he could call for the shadow again, Ed gave in to the tiredness and closed his heavy eyes.

Chapter 14

A shock at breakfast

Thud. Ed bolted upright in shock as the model earth that he and Sam had made rolled off the window sill and hit him right on top of his head. He opened his eyes and groaned as he rubbed the pain. Voices came from downstairs.

"What time is it?" Ed murmured. "Shadow?" He looked down at his waist and noticed that the remaining token and belt had gone. He rubbed his eyes as everything around him began to look as clear as day.

"The belt is gone, does this mean I stay here now, Shadow?" he called.

He climbed out of bed in search of the shadow. As he reached the bottom step, he turned and walked through the hall in the direction of the voices that were coming from the kitchen. His mum, dad, and brother were all sitting at the table, rushing down their breakfast and discussing where they were going to start searching today.

They never have breakfast together, Ed thought. At least his family had come together even if he could never truly be a part of it. He felt a sense of happiness at seeing them all sitting together and wished so much that he could be a part of it. His mum was frantically sorting a pile of the 'missing' flyers Ed had seen Jack giving out the day before, when his dad suddenly glanced up and looked straight in the direction of Ed.

His mouth widened, and he dropped the spoon that was balanced in his hand. Ed's mum peered up to see what the noise was and followed the fixed stare. Ed turned around to see if anything or anyone was behind him, but no.

"ED!" his mum screamed.

The whole family jumped up from their chairs and darted over to Ed in disbelief. Ed stood, surrounded by his family, being hugged, kissed, and feeling very confused. He patted himself down and then touched Jack's arm and gave out a shocked yell. It was real; he was real. He was back! But how?

Remembering the shadow, he spun around to check on whether or not it had returned to its owner. Sure enough, at the back of his heels was his trusted outline staring back at him. He smiled.

"That was the last moment," he said aloud.

"The last what?" his mum asked curiously. Ed didn't answer, and his mum didn't waste time asking what he had meant. They just stood together, in comfortable silence.

And that was Ed's final, and most important, moment of all. The rest of the day was spent with his family, who obviously had many concerns and questions over Ed's disappearance. Mark, the police officer who was helping to find Ed, came to the house to ask him questions, too.

Ed apologised to the adults. On consideration, he decided that the ordinary realm wouldn't understand the realm of invisibility, and that the moments he had created were best kept to himself for now. So, he decided to tell his family most of the truth; that he had hidden around school, wandered through town, and sneaked into the cinema before scurrying home late and hiding in the den through fear of being told off. A believable tale, and one that received several moments of consequence and lectures from the grownups that Ed knew he quite rightly deserved. Besides, he understood that they were being delivered with unconditional love attached.

But what, you may be wondering, came of those extraordinary moments? What had become of Bradley

Bellua and Maggie Bas? What, in fact, did the shadow do when instructed to alter the course of Mr Uset's work, and Mr Dion's evening? As magical as Ed transporting into the realm of invisibility was, as magical as the glistening tokens were, the real magic was yet to be realised.

Chapter 15

The extraordinarily magical days

A few days passed by from these extraordinary events, and the Usets spent time as a family. When he had stood surrounded by the people he loved the most, all talking around him; after seeing just how his disappearance had affected his family, Ed had made the decision to keep the realm of invisibility to himself. Besides, he didn't actually think that he'd be believed even if he did tell them the truth of the realms.

As for his wonder about the newspaper advert he saw when leaving Brad's house on 'that day,' it came to light that two days after Ed was back, his dad went for an interview for the job and was offered the position right there on the spot. It wasn't his own business, and Ed wouldn't get to spend the holidays in the workshop with his dad, but his dad was happier, and to Ed, that was enough for now.

It wasn't until Ed returned to school a few days later that he finally understood the moment that his shadow had created when he saw Brad alone in his room. Walking down the corridor to the library one rainy break time, Ed passed a classroom with a door that was ever so slightly ajar. Thinking it was just another empty room, he continued to walk until he heard the familiar voice of Brad, followed by Mr Dion. Assuming this was just another telling off for Brad, Ed listened in, feeling concerned after what he had seen at Brad's house. After a few minutes of eavesdropping, Mr Dion could be heard speaking in a soft tone.

"So, after I received the letter from your dad detailing your home situation, obviously we met with you and your dad yesterday, and I feel like we've made definite progress. How do you feel Brad?"

"Yeah, good. I liked chatting with Dad when you were

there, and I'm excited that you're going to help me see my mum. I don't know, I had a feeling in my stomach I couldn't get rid of, but now Dad has listened it's stopped a little bit," Brad said.

Ed knew all too well the feeling that Brad was trying to explain.

After standing and listening to what the shadow had created, a huge grin spread across Ed's face, and a strange, unusual feeling rippled across his stomach. Not the ache, as you may have assumed, but a sense of butterflies. The type of feeling you get when you win the 100m sprint on sports day and everyone chants your name. Ed hadn't always liked Brad, and he didn't understand him most of the time either, but in that moment it didn't matter. Mr Dion taking good care of Brad didn't anger Ed or make him frustrated, and it didn't take anything away from Ed. It made him glad. Besides, when Ed and his mum finally got the evening together that she had promised, she explained to her son just how much Mr Dion and the school had helped in searching for him.

One person who became quite significant in Ed's life after just one small moment on 'that day' was Maggie Bas. On the same day that Ed heard Mr Dion and Brad talking, he was on his way to the library, in search of Maggie. The pair met, coincidentally Maggie assumed, when scrolling through the non-fiction section and landing on the same book at the very same moment. After introducing himself to the quiet figure, the pair then spent the rest of the day meeting up at break time and lunchtime, and later discovered they didn't live all that far apart from each other. Ed knew, a while before Maggie, that he had found a friend for life and would make every moment count. Unlike Ed, Maggie was an avid cricketer but had always been too shy to join a team. Ed's newfound confidence and zest for life, mixed with Maggie's natural cricketing talent, resulted in the pair agreeing to join a team together that met every Tuesday evening; his new favourite day of the week.

Jack and Ed became much closer on Ed's return. He spent more time at home, met Ed to walk home from school the short route at the end of every day, and started teaching Ed how to play the guitar. To this day, they still fall out over whether or not Ed has snuck into his brother's room and touched his prized possessions, but that, Ed knew, would never change.

One night, after the excitement of re-entering the ordinary realm and meeting Maggie, Ed was sitting in his room about to settle down for a quiet evening of gaming, when he looked towards an old set of drawers opposite the den. Stood on top in a blue and white striped frame was a photograph of Ed and Sam, smiling. Ed was inside the rocket go-kart that his dad had made, and Sam was clinging onto the back. In that second, he knew there was one moment he was yet to create. That night, whilst in the den, it wasn't his game that he spent his evening on, but instead he sat and penned a letter to Sam, finally remembering the one person who he knew he could tell all about the realm of invisibility and the shadow that talked. He wrote and then sealed the letter, paused for a moment, and smiled. Life wasn't exactly how he would like it to be, but he had started to create his own moments, and he now knew the power of a single moment very well. Sure enough, a few days later, he received a moment in the post when he read and re-read (for what felt like a thousand times), a letter from Sam.

Dear Ed,

I thought maybe you had lost my address for a while! Miss you buddy. My new school is okay, not as good without you, but I've met some pretty cool people who I can't wait for you to meet when you come over and visit. I can't believe the invisibility thing! Did your shadow have a voice like Darth Vader? Because that's how I've imagined it in my head! What did you do? You need to tell me more about the belt and the tokens. I'd give anything for a magic belt! What's it like to vanish? Could you walk through doors? Anyway, I'm just glad you're back again and didn't disappear for good because I need you. Don't forget the earth model; you can bring it with you when you come! How is school? Maggie sounds cool; I think I remember seeing her a few times when we sat in the library. What else have you been up to? My mum said that in the next school holidays you can come and stay with us for the whole week! Let me know if you can come; I can't wait to see you!

Sam.

So, there you have it. You know the whole story: the realm, the shadow, and the token moments.

But what about today? What about right now? Well, you're about to be let into the present-day life of Edward Uset, for just a single moment before you go. The boy who once had an ache in his stomach now creates his own magic and looks for happiness in not-so-happy places. Come with me...

It starts on a Tuesday evening, with Ed closing the front

door and setting off to meet Maggie, cricket clothes in a rucksack clinging to his back. He walks forward, head up and smiling. Then Ed sees an all too familiar figure moving towards him. Its shadow is tall with messy hair. Bradley Bellua, dressed head to toe in his cricket whites is walking towards Ed.

"Hey, Ed, you okay?" Brad asks. Ed looks straight at Brad and pulls a small, unsure smile.

"Yes, thanks. You heading to cricket practice?"

"Yeah, well my mum has come to pick me up. She's taking me out for tea after. We just wondered if you wanted a lift? Peter is in the car, too. We can pick Maggie up on the next corner." Brad said in a rushed tone.

Ed saw how much effort it had taken Brad to come up to him and talk, and he noticed Brad taking deep breaths, almost like he was too nervous to ask. Ed took a deep breath and smiled as he leaned over Brad's shoulder and spotted Peter Tapper waving in the back seat of the humming car.

"Sure, that'd be great. Thanks," he replied.

The two boys walked off together towards Brad's mum who was waiting patiently in the driving seat, chatting to Peter. They aren't best friends; they don't spend evenings in each other's company, nor do they magically have things in common now, but they are friendly, and Ed is happy with that. Ed turns around for a single moment, just to check on something. Sure enough, beyond his loyal shadow that is sewn tightly to his heels, stands his mum and dad waving him off through the downstairs window. He looks down at his shadow and smiles,

"Unconditional love never stops," he whispers.

So, wherever you have been, or wherever you will go,

remember this story; the one of the boy with the magical moments. And if you, like Ed, should ever find yourself with an ache in the deepest, darkest pit of your stomach, caused by a moment that has made you feel terribly sad, worried, or angry, then turn around, spot your shadow, take a deep breath and make that moment magic.

Footnote

If you were wondering where the names of the characters in Invisible Ed came from, here's the answer!

Ed **Uset** – Danish meaning 'unseen'

Sam **Cara** – Gaelic meaning 'friend'

Brad **Bellua** – Latin meaning 'beast'

Peter **Tapper** – Norwegian meaning 'valiant'

Notes

Notes